LOOK OUT FOR THE WHOLE SERIES!

THE CASE OF THE
STINKY SMELL

**Hodder
Children's
Books**

A division of Hachette Children's Books

Special thanks to Lucy Courtenay and Artful Doodlers

Copyright © 2008 Chorion Rights Limited, a Chorion company

First published in Great Britain in 2008 by Hodder Children's Books

1

A Catalogue record for this book is available from the British Library

ISBN 978 0 340 95980 0

Typeset in Weiss by Avon DataSet Ltd,
Bidford on Avon, Warwickshire

Printed in Great Britain by
Clays Ltd, St Ives plc

The paper and board used in this paperback by Hodder Children's
Books are natural recyclable products made from wood grown in
sustainable forests. The manufacturing processes conform to the
environmental regulations of the country of origin.

Hodder Children's Books
a division of Hachette Children's Books
338 Euston Road, London NW1 3BH
An Hachette Livre UK Company
www.hachettelivre.co.uk

Chapter One

Through the lens of a hand-held video camera, the sun could be seen glittering on the vast expanse of sea. It glittered a bit more. A couple of tiny waves dipped and quivered, before the sea fell still again.

"Well," said Dylan from behind the camera. "This isn't as exciting as I'd hoped."

"Max is setting the *underwater* swimming record," Jo reminded her cousin. She checked her stopwatch, then patted her bored-looking dog Timmy gently on the head. "It's not that visual."

A little way along the beach, Allie – Jo and Dylan's American cousin – was doing a cheerleading routine, her shiny blond hair bouncing perfectly on her shoulders. "Break the record Max will do," she shouted, "he'll hold his breath and swim far, too!" Realising that Max couldn't hear her, she knelt down and yelled at the water: "Go, Max, go!"

Timmy, excited by Allie's display of enthusiasm, bounded away from Jo and barked encouragement at the waves as well.

"Jo," said Dylan, lowering his camera, "give me the sandwich bag. Allie, give me your scrunchy."

Allie handed her scrunchy over reluctantly. "It's not the best colour for you," she advised. "Kind of makes you look pale."

Dylan took the plastic sandwich bag from Jo and the elastic hair scrunchy from Allie. He wrapped the videocamera in the bag. Then, using his tripod, he thrust the camera under the water.

Under the waves, Max thrashed on with determination, his face bulging with the effort of holding his breath. He noticed the camera and gave it a cheerful thumbs-up before continuing on his way.

Swimming on Max's tail came a large, dim-witted fish. It approached the camera, studied it for a moment, opened its mouth wide and swallowed it whole.

Dylan felt the tug on his tripod. He whipped the tripod up out of the water like a fishing rod, pulling up the fish with it. The fish fell off on to the beach and flopped around for a bit until Timmy sniffed it and pushed it back into the water.

Drama over, Jo returned her gaze to the stopwatch. She glanced intently at the water. "He's getting closer . . ." she began.

BOOOOMMMM!

Water erupted from the sea in a giant geyser, accompanied by smoke and flames. Jo, Allie, Dylan and Timmy stumbled back from the shore in shock.

"I hope he wasn't underwater so long he burst!" Dylan said in dismay, his glasses splattered by the spray.

They looked towards the foaming water in consternation. Max arose in the midst of the disturbance, his blond hair plastered down on his head and an excited look on his face.

"Did you see that?" Max shouted, wading ashore. "It's like the world's biggest whale burped!"

The water fizzed in Max's wake, bubbling and smoking like a witch's cauldron. This was no whale. Something much more serious was going on.

Chapter Two

Being a small town, Falcongate didn't stretch to much in the way of TV news. As a result, "Falcongate 2 News Team" – comprising young reporter Polly Lucas and her wild chimpanzee partner Prince Extremely Hairy – shared space with the town bakery. This was handy if you both had some news and fancied an iced bun, but it wasn't the most comfortable arrangement in the world.

Inside the building, the two businesses were separated by a yellow line on the floor. Prince Extremely Hairy was waiting in line at the bakery counter, clutching his number ticket impatiently, while Polly Lucas tried to write a couple of reports on a desk the size of a biscuit tin in her cramped little cubicle.

"Number ninety-one," said the baker in a nasal sort of voice.

Prince Extremely Hairy looked at his ticket. Number ninety-seven. He screeched with irritation.

The doorbell tinkled, and the Five walked in. They made their way through the bakery and over to Polly's desk.

"Mmmm tarts . . ." Max mumbled, having a little trouble getting past the delicious-looking pastries. "Jam tarts . . ."

Jo steered him away from the bakery counter and on towards Polly.

"Miss Lucas," said Allie in excitement, "we have a big news story for you. Max set the breath-holding record! A minute fifty-eight seconds!"

"Actually, we have *two* stories," Jo said. "There was this really strange explosion . . ."

"*Actually,*" Dylan interrupted, "we have *three* stories." Ignoring his cousins' glare, he pressed on. "I've decided to become an internationally famous magician. It's good human interest stuff, and those guys make a load of loot."

To illustrate, Dylan held up a red ball in one hand. He placed another red ball in Polly's hand and then cleared his throat.

"Behold!" he began in his best magician's voice. "The ball in my hand will disappear and reappear in your hand!" He pulled a wand from somewhere and tapped his hand importantly. Then he opened it.

"The ball in my hand is still there," he said, looking confused. He glanced at Polly. "And the ball in your hand . . . ?"

Polly opened her hand.

"Was supposed to be my lunch," Dylan concluded, staring in disappointment at the squashed tomato lying in Polly's palm. "I really should read the directions before I try this stuff."

Polly put the squashed tomato down and turned to Max. "I'm afraid a minute fifty-eight only ties with the existing record, held by Lanny 'the Lung' Hafthorrson, a professional tuba player and balloon-animal artist," she said apologetically.

"Number ninety-two?" floated towards the Five from the bakery counter, followed by another impatient screech from Prince Extremely Hairy.

"What about the explosion?" Jo asked Polly. "The sea doesn't blow up every day."

"And we've ruled out whales burping and Max popping as the cause," Allie added.

"I'll check on that first thing tomorrow," Polly promised. "But today I've promised my boss two stories that require every ounce of my journalistic concentration."

Max looked impressed. "Wow," he breathed. "War breaking out? Big government scandal?"

"The mayor's cutting a ribbon, and some people are painting their house," Polly explained.

The Five tried but could not help looking unimpressed.

"I'd like to re-pitch the 'young magician' story," Dylan offered into the silence. "Pick a card . . ." He tried to fan a deck of cards, but they exploded out of his grip and flew everywhere.

"The mayor is opening the new bank vault," said Polly, gathering her things. "It's impenetrable. And Gaylord and Prunella Vanowen are restoring the oldest house in town."

"Oooh, could I come?" Allie begged. "I love old houses! And it would be neat to see the mayor! And

8

I bet I could learn a lot of career-woman professional-type stuff from you," she added, sensing Polly weakening. "Like being 'empowered', whatever that is. I hear it's good."

"Number ninety-three?" sniffed the baker in the background.

"C'mon Prince Extremely Hairy," Polly said to the chimp who was now hopping up and down in fury in front of the bakery counter. "We've got to get going."

Prince Extremely Hairy screeched in anger, grabbed handfuls of buns and cakes off the counter and started flinging them as hard as he could. Pies, muffins and bread flew through the air.

"First tip," said Polly to Allie as she dodged a bread roll, "don't have a chimp for a partner. C'mon – let's go."

"Mmmm," said Max happily, getting pelted with fairy cakes and tasting everything that came within reach of his tongue. "Throw some lemon cream . . ."

Polly and the Five struggled out of the bakery, keeping low and wiping chocolate icing off their faces.

"Prince Extremely Hairy has a good arm," said Jo

as they emerged at last into the street. "He'd make a good fast bowler if he wasn't insane and foul-smelling."

A rotten stink floated towards them from a nearby storm drain.

Dylan sniffed and wrinkled his nose. "Speaking of foul-smelling . . ."

Timmy made a sudden grab for Max as he was about to step over the drain. Seizing the seat of Max's trousers, Timmy yanked him backwards.

"Whoooah!" Max shouted, taken by surprise.

WHOOOSH!

A burst of flame and smoke belched from the drain. The flames shot underneath a car parked nearby, causing an explosion which tossed the car three metres straight up into the air. The vehicle promptly did two somersaults before landing back on all four wheels with a thud, the screech of a car alarm and the *pffft* of rapidly inflating airbags.

"At least it's still in one piece," Dylan said.

As they watched, the car's doors, bonnet and boot popped off, its wheels collapsed and its hubcaps rolled away down the street.

"OK," Dylan amended, "ten pieces."

Jo whistled. "All right," she said. "Unless there's a whale burping in the sewer, I think these explosions are a big story."

"A whale burping in the sewer would be a pretty good scoop too," Max pointed out as they stared at the wreckage lying in the road.

And even Jo had to agree on that one.

Chapter Three

Back at Jo's house, she and Timmy hurried into George's study with the boys. It was a higgledy-piggledy room, most surfaces scattered with books and papers and the walls decorated with botanical prints.

Jo went straight to the bookcase and pulled out a reference book. "There's got to be something in one of these books about what causes gas explosions," she explained, flicking through the pages.

"Eating too many beans usually does it for me," Dylan smirked.

Jo gave him an exasperated glance.

"I'm an eleven year-old boy," Dylan protested, raising his hands. "This kind of thing amuses me."

Dylan crossed to the bookcase. Reaching past Jo, he moved a book halfway out of the shelf. A little door clicked and swung open, revealing a magic book, a wand and a top hat.

"Whoa, secret compartment," said Max as Dylan pulled out the book and the hat. "How'd'you find that?"

Dylan shrugged. "I was looking for spare change, sweets, anything I could sell."

"There're secret nooks and crannies all over this house," Jo said, pushing the compartment shut again. "My mum says it was once owned by a magician."

"That's cool," Max sighed. A vague-looking expression floated across his face. "My dad says a hedgehog once lived in our attic."

Dylan tapped the wand on to his hat. "Want to see me pull a rabbit out of my hat?" he asked the others hopefully.

"Rabbit, hedgehog, elephant, whatever . . ." Jo said, still engrossed in her reference book.

Dylan read from his magic book as Max and

Timmy watched him eagerly. He put down the book, cleared his throat and tapped the hat again.

"According to this," Dylan said, "I just tap my wand and say the magic words. 'Prest-o change-o! Rabbit-o!'"

Instead of a rabbit, a flash of fire and smoke burst from the hat. The others coughed and waved their hands in front of their faces as a stink drifted across the room.

"Uh-oh!" said Dylan.

"Phew!" Max said, looking revolted by the stench. "That's what the sea smelled like when it exploded."

"It's what the storm-drain explosion smelled like, too," Jo said, her brow creasing. "Like rotten eggs."

"I'd blamed that smell on Timmy, but maybe I was wrong," said Dylan, laying the smoking hat on George's desk.

Timmy glared at him, offended.

"I told you – I'm eleven," Dylan said defensively. "This stuff cracks me up."

Jo had returned to her book, and was now flicking through the pages purposefully. She reached the page she was looking for and jabbed it with her finger. "It says here that methane gas smells like rotting vegetable matter," she said in triumph. "And it's very explosive." Then she frowned. "But why is methane gas exploding around town?"

"Why is *anything* exploding in Dylan's hat?" Max added.

Dylan studied his magic book. "Oh, I see," he said at last. "The pages were stuck together. I wasn't doing the appearing rabbit trick, I was doing the exploding hat trick."

Jo grinned. "Well, at least it wasn't the exploding rabbit trick."

Across the town, in the untidy garden in front of a decrepit old mansion, a rabbit was munching peacefully on some grass. To the untrained eye, it appeared to explode as a puff of flame and smelly smoke shot out of a nearby rabbit hole and threw the rabbit into the air. It landed, shaken but unharmed, and hopped away unsteadily.

Meanwhile, Allie, Polly and Prince Extremely Hairy were making their way up the mansion's broken path to the front door, stepping past piles of rubble, boards, tools, buckets and other assorted building materials on the way. Unable to resist, Prince Extremely Hairy leaped on to a nearby mound of earth and beat his chest importantly. The whole house was rumbling, as some kind of drilling equipment pounded away inside.

"I bet they're putting in granite countertops," Allie said happily. "In Malibu, if you don't have granite countertops, people won't even look at you."

Polly had to knock several times before she was

heard. The rumbling stopped. A moment later, the door opened to reveal a young couple in their twenties. They managed to look posh even though they were covered in dirt, and were wearing overalls and work boots.

"Hi," Polly began, trying to peer inside the house. "Polly Lucas, News Two. Your restoration is big news, and I'm here to get the inside story."

"Oh, bung-ho, Miss Lucas!" said Gaylord Vanowen, his voice absurdly posh. "Jolly nice to meet you. Bad timing, though – you've caught us at a bally inopportune moment."

"We are, I fear, it seems, as it were, indisposed," added his wife Prunella Vanowen, her voice even posher than her husband's.

The man tried to shut the door, but Polly put her foot in the way. "Won't take a jiffy," Polly said firmly. "The people of Falcongate are curious."

"They are," Allie added. "They really like to know what's going on."

The woman's expression hardened. "And we simply crave the chance to quench their curiosity," she said, "but as Jane Austen so deftly put it in *Mansfield Park* – 'Go away'."

17

"Right after we've got our story," Polly said. " We can't wait to see what you're doing with the place."

The reporter pushed her way inside. Allie followed as the Vanowens reluctantly allowed them through.

Chapter Four

Once inside, it was hard not to notice that there was no restoration work going on at all. The place was almost empty. There was no sign of the loud rumbling equipment either.

"You're not doing *anything* with the place," said Allie in disappointment, staring around at the old wallpaper and tattered carpet.

"That's workmen for you, eh, what?" said Gaylord Vanowen with a forced laugh. "Delivered *all* of our furniture and what-have-you to Falcon*ford*, and we're in Falcon*gate*. Silly, really. Ha, ha, ha!"

Allie looked more cheerful. "When you do get

your stuff, are you going with drapes or shutters?" she asked eagerly.

"Curtains . . ." said Gaylord Vanowen.

"Shutters," said Prunella at the same time.

"Shutters," Gaylord said quickly, just as Prunella said: "Curtains."

"The point is," Gaylord hurried on, glancing at his wife, "we haven't arrived at a meeting of the minds in regard to the windows yet."

Polly looked around. "I'm a trained reporter, Mr Vanowen," she said suspiciously, "and I have to say I sense something a little fishy here."

"Ha, ha," said Gaylord. His eyes darted helplessly around the room for a change of subject, and alighted on Prince Extremely Hairy. "What a frightfully adorable ape," he said in relief. "Really smashing."

Prince Extremely Hairy stopped peeling strips of old wallpaper off the wall and leaped on to Gaylord's head, where he clung like an enormous and unflattering hat.

"Oy," Gaylord yelled, all evidence of a posh accent dropping away like a stone. "The bloomin' hairbag's going for my eyes! Grab him!"

"Forget the monkey," snarled Prunella, her accent collapsing in a heap as well. "Grab *them!*"

Prunella grabbed Polly by the arm, but Allie ducked successfully away from Gaylord's grasp. As Prince Extremely Hairy leaped up to a dusty chandelier and started swinging from it, Allie raced towards the front of the house, pursued by Gaylord.

"I've heard house restoration is stressful, but this is crazy," Allie shouted, glancing fearfully over her shoulder. She ran through the dining room into the kitchen, where a stable-style door separated the two rooms. She swung round and slammed the top half of the stable door, which walloped into Gaylord's head.

"Owfff," Gaylord grunted, sprawling on to his back.

Allie looked quickly around the kitchen, and spotted an old dumb-waiter in the corner. She opened the door, climbed inside and started desperately hoisting it up.

"She's taking the dumb-waiter upstairs!" Gaylord called to Prunella as he got groggily to his feet. "I'll head her off!"

He raced to a flight of stairs leading off the

kitchen and ran up them two at a time. Allie waited for half a second, then lowered herself back to the kitchen.

"Psych," she grinned to herself, climbing out of the dumb-waiter and heading for the kitchen window.

"She's still down here, you fool!" Prunella yelled to her husband as she continued struggling with Polly.

In a blur of matted brown fur, Prince Extremely Hairy bounded into the kitchen and boosted Allie out of the window, just as Gaylord hurried back down the stairs. Gaylord reached through the window to try to grab Allie, but Prince Hairy blew a raspberry, leaped to the top of the window and used his weight to slam it down on Gaylord's back.

Gasping from her near escape, Allie ran round to the front of the house. Gaylord burst through the front door after her.

"Where d'you think you're going, you brat?" Gaylord panted.

Allie ran up one of the mounds of earth outside the front door and stepped on a wooden plank, catapulting a bucket through the air and on to Gaylord's head.

"Whoohoohoo!" she shouted gleefully, looking back and lifting her arms in triumph as Prince Extremely Hairy leaped on to the bucket and started pounding it like a drum. With a roar of fury, Gaylord Vanowen shook off both the bucket and the chimpanzee. Prince Hairy immediately swung up a tree.

Allie raced to the edge of the property. "If I break a nail after all this, it'll be really sad," she muttered, vaulting the fence.

As Allie landed on the other side, a pair of hands shot out and grabbed her.

"We may not know much about restoration," Prunella snarled as Allie struggled, "but we know how to deal with bratty kids who poke their noses where they don't belong."

And she hustled Allie back towards the house.

Chapter Five

Back in George's study, Max and Jo entered with their arms full of old books and plans. Ignoring them, Dylan got a little more comfortable in his chair and stuck his nose deeper into his magic book.

"Hey, Dylan," Jo said, dumping the books and plans on George's desk. "Allie back yet?"

"Not yet," Dylan murmured. "But you know how she gets about wallpaper. Loses all track of time."

Max waved his blueprints at Dylan. "We checked out all these records at the Town Hall. Turns out there's pockets of methane gas all over this area," he said.

"Mmm-hmmm," Dylan mumbled, turning a page. "That's nice . . ." He looked up at last, and waved his book vaguely at Jo and Max. "I sawed Aunt George in half, but I can't quite work out how to get her back together," he explained.

Across the room, George's head protruded from one half of a Saw-A-Man-In-Half cabinet. The other half of the cabinet contained her feet, and was halfway across the room.

"Hel-lo!" George said cheerfully.

"Here," Max offered, setting down his plans. "I'll help . . ."

"No hurry, dear," said George as Dylan and Max wrestled to push the boxes back together. "If someone could just scratch my feet for me . . ."

"There's a big gas pocket near Otter's Point," Jo said, studying the plans she'd spread over the desk. "I bet that's what the sea explosion was."

"No," Dylan was saying to Max as he struggled with his half of the cabinet, "I think that tab goes in that slot." He looked over his shoulder at Jo and asked: "And they're all starting to explode at once?"

"I think the first box shouldn't fit there until that tab pushes back," Max offered. "Or vice versa . . ."

He too turned to Jo. "We should call Polly Lucas, let her know about all this methane," he suggested.

Jo picked up the phone to call Polly. "Hello, Polly Lucas please?"

She winced and pulled the receiver from her ear as Polly's boss on the other end of the phone started shouting so loudly that Max, George and Dylan could hear him from across the room.

Jo pressed her ear gingerly to the receiver again. She listened, looking concerned, then covered the receiver with her hand.

"Polly's boss says she never came back to the studio," she told the others. She held the receiver to her ear again. "I know she's supposed to be at the opening of the new bank vault . . ." she said into the phone. "She's not there either? And the mayor's hopping mad?" She listened carefully. "Oh, he's just hopping," she said after a minute. "Well, that's his problem . . . Thank you."

Jo hung up the phone. "They're about to cut the ribbon at the vault," she told the others in a worried voice. "Maybe Allie will show up during the ceremony."

Jo switched on the study's TV. The screen

26

showed the mayor – a short, plump, jolly individual with a big quiff of hair – standing next to the heavy, shiny door of the new bank vault. The door stood open to display mountains of cash and coins inside, and a ceremonial ribbon stretched across the doorway.

". . . and our new vault door, once locked, will be impenetrable," the mayor was saying in a surprisingly high-pitched voice to a small gathering of spectators. "Not even some sort of superhero, be his powers derived from alien parentage or radioactive misadventure, could use some sort of laser-stare to breach the security of—"

BOOOMM!

The mayor was interrupted by an explosion of flame and smoke bursting through a heat vent, which knocked off his extravagant toupee and sent it flying through the air and straight into the arms of a lucky onlooker.

"My hair!" shouted the mayor in dismay.

"I don't like the look of this," said Jo, staring at the screen.

Max shuddered. "Me neither. Without his wig, the mayor looks like a watermelon with eyes."

"I mean Allie," Jo said impatiently. "Why haven't we heard from her? Why aren't she and Polly at the bank?"

"We could go to that old house they were going to," Max suggested. "Maybe they're still there."

"Just one second," Dylan puffed, standing up from fiddling around with the catch on the two Saw-A-Man-In-Half cabinet pieces. "I think I've got this . . ."

He opened the lid and helped George out. Oddly, Jo's mother had an arm where a leg was

28

supposed to be, and a leg where an arm was supposed to be.

"Well," Dylan said, studying George doubtfully, "you can get that sorted out."

"Or you could join the circus," Max added, ever helpful. His eyes glazed over as George looked at her misplaced limbs. "Mmmm, circus food!"

Chapter Six

The Vanowens' mansion loomed over the street, looking as decrepit and forbidding as ever. Max, Jo, Dylan and Timmy pushed their bikes up to the front door cautiously. The air was filled with the same rumbling sound that had puzzled Allie and Polly earlier.

Jo knocked on the door. After a moment, the rumbling noise stopped. Prunella Vanowen opened the door, looking irritated. When she saw the visitors, she quickly adjusted her face to a smile.

"Sorry to bother you," Jo said politely. "I think my cousin Allie was here earlier—"

"Oh, indeed!" Prunella interrupted, her voice

gushing. "With that lovely television reporter and her simian sidekick! They left ages ago! Tra-la!"

Jo, Max and Dylan tried to peer round Prunella to see inside the house. But Gaylord stepped into the doorframe, blocking their view.

"Of course one would love to chat," said Gaylord blandly, "but one does have painting to get on with. Special antique paint from the eighteen-hundreds, don't you know – dries in an instant, tricky to work with. Fine, then – tinkerty-tonk!"

Waving a cheerful farewell, he slammed the door shut.

"Did you notice anything odd about the Vanowens?" Jo said, turning slowly away from the door.

"Well, they were very polite," Max said.

"They said they were painting, but they didn't have a speck of paint on them," Jo said with a frown. "Remember when we painted the barn last year?"

Max snorted, reaching for his wallet. "I had so many spots I looked like a red leopard!" he chortled, producing a photo of himself covered in red blotches and showing it proudly to the others.

31

"Which is odd, because we painted the barn green," Dylan said, handing the photo back.

"I never did work that out," Max admitted, looking perplexed as he stared at the picture.

"Mr Vanowen's nails were filled with dirt," Jo continued. "How do you get dirty nails painting?"

"Painting dirty pictures?" Dylan offered.

They tried to peer through a window into the house. But Gaylord pulled a pair of curtains shut with a wink and a wave. Before they could scurry to the next window along, Prunella lowered the window's blinds with a wave. It was the same story at the next window, with Gaylord slamming a set of shutters with a cheerful thumbs-up.

"Well, I'm not Christmas carolling at *this* house," Max said grumpily. He brightened. "Ooh, Christmas – I hope I get a snowboard this year."

"I don't know if I buy this whole 'antique paint' thing," Jo said, shaking her head as they pushed their bikes back down the broken path to the street. "I want to find out the Vanowens' true colours . . ."

They cycled into the centre of Falcongate, heading for the town's single paint shop, and parked their bikes outside. Like most of Falcongate's shops, the place was small and cramped. The shop's owner Mr Crackler was standing on top of a ladder in the window, stacking a display of paint tins into a tall pyramid against a carefully arranged dustsheet.

"Mr Crackler," said Jo, keen to get straight to the point, "we'd like to talk to you about paint."

"A divine subject," said Mr Crackler happily from the top of his ladder. "The glory of civilization. Tool of Rembrandt. Where would we be without paint?"

"Pretty much in the same place," Max said. He frowned. "It would just be kind of . . . brown."

Jo hurried on. "Those new people in town, the Vanowens – they said they had paint from the eighteen-hundreds."

Mr Crackler snorted. "There is no such thing," he said. "It would have turned to dust while Churchill was still in nappies. Those Vanowens are pulling the dustsheet over your eyes."

Dylan eyed the dustsheet beneath the pyramid of paint tins. "Speaking of dustsheets," he said, cracking his knuckles, "check out *this* trick . . ."

He rolled up his sleeves, leaned down, grabbed

33

the dustsheet and pulled. Incredibly, he succeeded in pulling the cloth from beneath the pyramid of paint without a single wobble from the tins.

"Hey!" Dylan said in surprise. "I did it!"

"Yes," said Mr Crackler, frowning from his place at the top of the ladder. "But that sheet was glued to a loose floorboard . . ."

Dylan examined the underside of the dustsheet. It was still stuck to a chunk of wood.

"Which means I'm in trouble . . ." Mr Crackler squeaked.

CRRRAACCKK!

One leg of Mr Crackler's ladder sank through a hole in the floor. As the ladder gave way, Mr Crackler flung out his arms desperately, grabbing on to a hanging light for support. The light swung, carrying Mr Crackler straight through his pyramid of tins like a bowling ball in a skittle alley. Jets of multicoloured paint fountained through the air.

The kids backed out of the shop as Mr Crackler dangled helplessly from the lamp, covered with paint and spluttering.

"OK," said Dylan, moving rather fast down the street, "but theoretically, the trick *did* work . . ." He cleared his throat and changed the subject as they approached the new bank with its GRAND OPENING! banners and balloons. "So those Vanowens lied about paint. I guess good manners don't count for everything."

"Maybe it's a coincidence that the Vanowens show up in town just when these explosions start happening," said Jo thoughtfully. "But my gut says it isn't."

"My gut says it wants a sausage sarny," said Max.

Timmy stepped in front of them and growled.

"Timmy wants one, too," Dylan added.

Timmy growled again making the kids stop just short of a grate in the middle of the pavement. There was a familiar flash of smoke and flame from the grate, and a nearby dustbin was tossed high into the air. As the dustbin came down again, it landed in a wagon full of hay that was parked nearby, setting fire to the hay and sending the wagon trundling off down the sloping street.

Chapter Seven

Jo, Max and Dylan jumped on their bikes and pedalled in fierce pursuit of the burning wagon, swerving round scattering pedestrians. The flames from the blazing hay were already roaring so high that they were licking at the passing telephone wires as the wagon flew along. Racing beside the others as fast as his four legs would carry him, Timmy barked just in time to stop a lady with a pram from crossing the street directly in the path of the burning wagon.

As they pedalled past a sporting-goods shop, Jo snatched up a croquet mallet and ball from a pavement display. Dropping the ball, she whacked it with a mallet. The ball rocketed forward, hitting the rear wheel of the wagon and forcing it to change direction.

"Right on target," Max cheered, racing beside Jo. "Great shot!"

"Not to be a Negative Nelly," Dylan said, "but now it's heading for the petrol station."

The wagon was indeed trundling in the direction of a petrol station on the corner of the road.

"I wouldn't worry about that," Jo said, pulling her bike to a stop.

They watched the wagon mount the pavement and shear off a water hydrant. The water shot up and doused the flaming hay in a sizzle of steam.

"Ah," said Dylan, screeching his bike to a halt as Al Fresco Freddy, the town character, rushed out of a nearby alley and threw himself under the cascading water for an impromptu shower. "Well played."

"Jo," Max said, squealing to a halt beside Dylan, "what does your gut say about where Allie is?"

Jo addressed her midsection. "What do you think, gut?" She pushed her voice up a notch or two, pretending to be her own gut. *"Mwah, mwah, mrah-mrah-mrah."* Grinning, she looked at the others. "My gut thinks the Vanowens might know something . . ."

The Kirrins stealthily approached the Vanowens' house from the road, keeping down as low as they could.

"They don't seem to want us coming through the front door," Jo whispered. "I think we should respect that."

Jo, Max, Dylan and Timmy sneaked round to the back, where they spotted a beautiful stained-glass

window with a skylight in the roof above it. The skylight was open.

"Dylan," said Max, staring up at the skylight, which stood about seven metres above the ground. "I don't suppose you know the Indian Rope Trick."

"No," Dylan admitted. "But I know the Breaking-And-Entering Trick . . ."

He hunted around amidst the building supplies that littered the Vanowens' garden, and found a long extension cable and a heavy metal clamp. Knotting the cable to the clamp, Dylan eyed the distance up to the skylight. He started swinging the cable in small circles, building up some momentum. Finally, he let the clamp fly.

"Eeek," Dylan winced as the clamp missed the skylight by a mile and shattered the gorgeous stained-glass window instead, sending rainbow shards of glass flying everywhere. "Wow, I hope the Vanowens are guilty of *something* . . ."

Stealthily, they climbed through the now-empty window frame and dropped down into the house. The only sound was a deep rumbling noise coming from somewhere beneath their feet.

"Either your gut's talking," Max said to Jo, "or

there's something going on in the basement."

Timmy sniffed the floor energetically.

"What do you smell, Timmy?" Jo asked. "Is it Allie?"

Still snuffling at the ground, Timmy made his way to the cellar door. The others followed as he took off down the steps into the dark, damp cellar. Disappointingly, the room was empty except for some barrels and a few hams hanging from the rafters.

"I don't think the Timster smells Allie," Dylan guessed, watching as Timmy kept sniffing around. "He smells ham."

But Timmy wasn't sniffing upwards. His nose was firmly pressed to the bottom of the cellar steps. On closer inspection, Jo spotted a trapdoor set neatly in the floor.

"Or maybe he does smell Allie," Dylan said sheepishly as Jo heaved the trapdoor up, "and once again I've been less clever than a dog."

A ladder stretched down to a second cellar. Timmy jumped down and Max, Dylan and Jo followed down the ladder to investigate.

Allie, Polly and Prince Extremely Hairy were all

tied up and gagged in the middle of the floor.

"Ha!" said Jo triumphantly, patting her stomach. "Good going, gut."

"Don't worry, Allie," said Max, heading towards his cousin. "We'll have you out of here in no time."

As Max and Dylan untied Allie, she made urgent muffled sounds beneath her gag.

Dylan tugged the gag out of Allie's mouth. "What are you trying to tell us?" he asked.

"That the Vanowens are behind you!" Allie shouted frantically.

Max, Dylan and Jo whirled round to see Gaylord and Prunella Vanowen clutching crowbars and more rope. They were both standing in the mouth of a deep dark tunnel stretching away through the cellar wall, which Max, Dylan, Jo and Timmy had failed to notice.

"Well, well," smiled Gaylord Vanowen as he patted the crowbar in the palm of his hand. "Look who's here."

"Bad gut!" Jo scolded her stomach gloomily as the Vanowens seized them and started tying them up. "Bad gut . . ."

Chapter Eight

The Five, Polly and Prince Extremely Hairy were all hustled to the ground, and Gaylord started tying everyone up again. Still gagged, Polly and Prince Extremely Hairy looked sympathetically at the newcomers.

"That'll hold you brats till we get back," said Gaylord Vanowen, tightening the last knot on the ropes.

After making sure that their victims were secure, the villains headed on down the tunnel, where the Five could see an extraordinary digging machine. It looked like a dune buggy, with a huge drill-bit on the front and side-mounted scoops to move the freshly dug earth out of the way. Gaylord fired up the engine, which roared and rumbled like a hungry animal. Then he and Prunella drove off down the tunnel.

"This is in no way a statement of support for the Vanowens," said Dylan as he watched the tail lights of the buggy disappear, "but that is a very cool machine."

Jo wriggled to get more comfortable. "I guess that explains all the explosions lately," she said.

"I guess it does," Allie agreed. Then she frowned. "How does it do that?"

Looking just as confused as Allie, Polly made inquisitive sounds through her gag.

"There are pockets of methane gas all around here," Max explained. "They're setting off the explosions as they tunnel through them."

"The question is, where are they tunnelling?" Dylan asked. "I don't think they're just looking to avoid traffic . . ."

Jo glanced down the tunnel. "Well, they're heading southeast," she said. "That means roughly the crossroads at Church Road and the High Street."

43

"Let's see," Allie said, working it out. "There's a laundry there, and an ice-cream shop, and—"

"The bank!" everyone gasped together as the truth sank in.

Inside the bank, a guard was sitting outside the vault, reading a comic book. He heard a distant rumbling, considered it briefly, decided to ignore it and returned to his book.

Inside the vault itself, the digging machine burst up through the floor like a mechanical mole. The Vanowens climbed out of the machine and looked around.

"I always say, 'If you can't go through the door, go through the floor'," Gaylord gloated, rubbing his hands.

"And I always say, 'Shut up and start shovelling'," snapped Prunella.

She opened a huge sack. Gaylord grabbed a shovel and began scooping cash and coins inside.

"It's going to take a long time to count all this," Gaylord grunted, pouring gleaming piles of gold and silver into the sack.

"We won't count it," grinned Prunella as Gaylord continued shovelling. "We'll weigh it."

Back in the tunnel, the Five, Polly and Prince Extremely Hairy were still tied up. They had been discussing the Vanowens' daring robbery plan – although, admittedly, Polly hadn't been able to say anything useful through her gag, and Prince Extremely Hairy had spent the time hunting for fleas on his tummy.

"Pretty ingenious," Jo admitted. "Tunnel straight into the bank vault and clean it out. And we can't stop them."

"On the plus side, I don't feel at all bad about breaking their window," Dylan said.

The familiar rumble of the digging machine approached back through the tunnel.

The Vanowens stopped their outlandish vehicle and climbed out with their sacks of loot.

"Well, that was fun," Gaylord leered at the captives.

"I don't suppose it's occurred to you that you've left a trail straight here," said Max.

"That's right," Gaylord said, with a mock-worried face. "Guess we'd better give ourselves up, eh, Prunella?" He clicked his fingers, as if something inspired had just occurred to him. "Or, we could just destroy this house and tunnel and everything in it, and *not* leave a trail!"

"I vote for that," Prunella grinned.

Allie frowned. "But . . . *we're* in the tunnel."

"That's right," Gaylord said. "And there's a *big* methane pocket just about a hundred metres from here. I'll just send our little digging machine here in that direction . . ."

He paused just long enough for Jo to grasp the Vanowens' horrible plan. ". . . And turn it into a tunnelling bomb," she finished, staring at Gaylord in horror.

"Ding!" beamed Gaylord. "The pushy girl wins the prize. The prize is a free fireworks show, and you've got the best seats in the house!"

Chapter Nine

The Five glanced at each other in dismay. Polly and Prince Extremely Hairy struggled furiously with their bonds. Smirking, Gaylord Vanowen started the rumbling motor on the digging machine and sent it tunnelling away through the earth, straight towards the methane pocket.

"It's been ever so much fun," Gaylord said, resuming his oh-so-posh voice as he and Prunella headed back up the ladder to the cellar. "Cheerio!"

Helplessly, the captives watched the Vanowens clamber up the ladder and slam the trapdoor shut. This time, it really looked as if there was no way out.

"I've been working on one last magic trick since we've been down here," Dylan spoke into the silence. "And I think I've just about got it."

"Dylan, this is not the time for magic," Jo hissed, wrestling with the ropes round her wrists.

"You'll like this one," Dylan promised. "Ta-da!"

He pulled his hands from behind his back and waggled them in the air. Somehow, he had managed to untie himself.

"I'd applaud," Allie said weakly, "but my hands have been tied up for many hours."

"Good job, Dylan," Max enthused. "All those hours of practice finally paid off."

Dylan looked sheepish. "Actually," he admitted, "having my Scout knife is what paid off."

He held up his pocket knife, before using it to cut the others free. Allie shook her hands with energetic relief.

"Oh!" she groaned, shaking hard. "Feeling coming back to hands. Hands tingly!"

Polly yanked the gag out of her mouth as soon as Dylan had cut the ropes binding her hands. "I'll go and see if I can find help," she said, scrambling to her feet. "And a loo," she added, taking the ladder steps two at a time with Prince Extremely Hairy by her side: "We've been down here for*ever*."

"For our next trick," Jo said, flexing her numb fingers, "we need to find the tunnelling machine."

"Before it makes *us* disappear," said Max.

The Five ran down the freshly dug tunnel after the rumbling digger.

"I can hear it up ahead," Max shouted over his shoulder.

Allie started coughing. The others sniffed at the stink of rotten eggs that was starting to waft towards them. Timmy barked a warning.

"The air's getting unsafe to breathe," Jo choked, her eyes beginning to stream.

"In minutes the machine's going to hit and we're all KABOOM!" Dylan said in horror. "Our fingerprints won't even be left."

"Well, thanks for that visual, Dylan," Allie said grimly.

Heaving for breath, the Five stopped and stared at each other.

"You guys go back," Max said. "I can catch the machine."

"But there's no air to breathe," Jo pointed out.

"What better time to break the breath-holding record?" Max said with a grin. He took a massive deep breath, held it, gave his cousins the thumbs-up and plunged down the stinking tunnel after the digging machine.

Moments later, Allie, Dylan, Jo and Timmy hurried out of the Vanowens' front door. The air smelt sweet and fresh after the eggy stink underground.

Jo counted off the seconds on her watch. "He's been down there nearly two minutes," she told the others as they stopped on the pavement and looked back at the house.

"What if he doesn't make it?" Allie asked, her bottom lip trembling.

Dylan ticked off the order of events on his fingers. "The ground will rumble, Timmy will bark because he smells gas, and there will be a very big explosion right where we're standing."

"Two minutes," said Jo tensely, staring at her watch again. "Two-oh-one . . . Two-oh-two . . ."

The ground rumbled warningly. Timmy barked. As the kids braced themselves for an explosion, the earth fountained up in front of them and Max rocketed to the surface behind the driving wheel of the digging machine, spitting dirt and grinning from ear to ear.

"Any messages for me while I was gone?" he said jauntily as he got his breath back.

"I've got a message for you," Jo said in delight. "Let's catch the Vanowens. They're heading out towards Old Road. They can't have gone very far."

Max revved the digging machine. "Can I offer anyone a lift?" he asked.

Chapter Ten

Everyone hopped up on to the digging machine behind Max. With a roar of the rumbly engine, Max turned the vehicle away from the road.

"Isn't it the other way?" Allie shouted over the racket as they bumped across the Vanowens' garden.

"Yeah," Max nodded, steering expertly through the mounds of rubble and building junk. "What's your point?"

Aiming at the stone wall around the Vanowens' property, Max drove the machine straight onwards. The drill-bit on the machine burrowed through the stone like butter.

The cows in the field beyond the stone wall stopped mid-chew as the vehicle thundered past them. It flattened everything in its path: ripping through a haystack, then a hedge, and finally tearing right through the middle of a billboard standing on the edge of a road – along which the Vanowens happened to be driving at that very moment.

"It's those kids!" Prunella gasped, grabbing Gaylord's arm as they drove at breakneck speed towards the tattered billboard and the digger. "Look out!"

53

Swearing loudly, Gaylord swerved the car away from the Kirrins and on to a side road, which wound round a small hill.

"Hands inside the vehicle, everyone . . ." Max advised in a fatherly tone of voice. He swung the wheel of the digging machine and ploughed the vehicle straight into the hill, where it disappeared into the earth as if – as Dylan would have put it – by magic.

Gaylord pressed hard on the accelerator as Prunella looked over her shoulder. "Looks like you lost them," she said in satisfaction, staring at the empty road behind them. "We're going to get away—"

Their car slewed sideways and plummeted straight into a sinkhole which had opened up in the road just in front of them. The digging machine, still driven by Max, burst up out of the ground alongside the road.

"I'll say it again," Dylan grinned, watching as the defeated Vanowens slumped over in their wrecked car, "this is a *very* cool machine."

Half an hour later, the Five watched from the verge

as Constable Lily Stubblefield of the Falcongate Police Constabulary handcuffed Gaylord and Prunella and led them away, watched by the Falcongate 2 News camera.

"Good work, young Kirrins," Constable Stubblefield called over her shoulder, chuckling: "I should put you on the police payroll!" Then she paused. "I'm not serious," she warned. "Don't ask for money."

Polly Lucas approached Max with a microphone in her hand.

"Max, can I ask a couple of quick questions?" she said, thrusting the microphone towards Max.

"Oh, you want to see how I held my breath?" Max said, looking pleased. "Like this . . ."

"No," Polly said as Max took a deep breath and started holding it, "I . . ."

"This seems like a good time for a little hocus-pocus," Dylan butted into Polly's camera shot. "I have here an ordinary top hat. I crack an ordinary egg therein . . ." He demonstrated – "And presto change-o . . ."

A flock of pigeons darted out of the hat, swarmed around Dylan and started pecking him hard.

"Aaagghh!" Dylan squealed, flinging his hands over his head to protect himself.

Jumping up at the birds in excitement, Timmy barked furiously and chased every feather he could see.

"Timmy!" Jo shouted, running over and trying to calm down her dog. "Down boy! Timmy!"

Allie poked her head into the camera's view. "Hi, Aunt George!" she waved cheerfully at Polly's camera. "Hi, Uncle Ravi! Hi, Aunt George! Hi!"

Polly Lucas forced her way to the front of the shot through the whirling chaos. "From Falcongate, this is Polly Lucas," she panted, "with the Kirrin kids and Timmy. In this reporter's opinion, they're all going to be famous . . ."

Epilogue

Back in George's study later that day, Dylan aimed his video camera at the homely scene before him. Allie was curled up in a chair, reading a magazine. Max and Jo were playing draughts by the fire, with Timmy curled at Jo's feet.

"Sticky Situation Number One Hundred and Eight: You Smell Gas," cued Dylan.

Max sniffed theatrically. "I smell gas," he announced.

The others looked at each other. There *was* a gassy smell. Their carefully rehearsed script suddenly took on new meaning.

Allie fanned her magazine. "Any qualified movie

star or celebrity chef will tell you," she said, "if you smell gas, open all your windows . . ."

Jo jumped up and flung open the study windows.

"Put out any flames or sparks in the house . . ." Allie continued.

Max leaned over the fireplace and quickly threw handfuls of sand into the grate to put the fire out.

"Then get out of the house and call your local gas company," said Allie, getting up rather quickly.

Still filming, Dylan followed the others, trying to keep his camera still while fanning the air with his free hand. Allie had already pulled out her mobile phone and was making an urgent call.

"Hello, gas company?" she said. "I'd like to report a strong, unpleasant odour in our house . . ."

The kitchen window swung open. The smell got worse.

"No need to call the gas company, dears," George called out of the window, looking a little hot and dishevelled. "I'm just cooking my famous kidney, liver and broccoli soup."

The Five exchanged panicked looks.

"Sticky Situation One Hundred and Nine," Dylan muttered: "Your Aunt Makes Stinky Soup."

"Gas company?" Allie said quickly into the phone. "You'd better come anyway. There's some delicious soup for you to eat. Mmm, soup!"

She hung up, looking a little pale. "Let's get out of here!" she advised the others.

And the Famous Five fled down the garden and out of sight.

THE CASE OF THE
DEFECTIVE DETECTIVE

Read on for
Chapter One of the
Famous 5's next
Case File . . .

*Hodder
Children's
Books*

A division of Hachette Children's Books

Chapter One

Apart from the fact that everything was upside-down, it was a normal evening in the study at Jo's house.

Timmy the dog was playing with a knotted rope beside the fire as it flickered comfortably in the grate. Jo was building a house of cards, her dark hair falling across her face as she concentrated on balancing the cards just right. Allie was sitting in an armchair, engrossed in her glossy fashion and gossip magazine. And Max was hanging from the bookcase with his digital camera pressed to his face. Hence the upside-down part.

"Nope . . ." Max fiddled with his focus, his blond

hair hanging down as he zoomed from one cousin to the next. "Nope . . . Nope . . ."

"Max," said Allie in exasperation, laying down her magazine and turning to face the camera, "how do you expect me to learn how movie stars plan to save the environment when you're hanging around like a paparazzi possum?" She paused, brightening. "Oooh!" she said thoughtfully. "That'd be a good cartoon character!"

"It's my photography class project," Max explained, still hanging upside down. "*One Hundred Photos – Strange, Interesting or Beautiful.*"

"Ooh," said Allie, immediately keen. "Take my picture!"

She rushed out to the coat rack in the hallway and grabbed a hat and feather boa to use as props, before returning to strike a series of model poses.

Jo glanced up from her card-house and winced. 'That definitely counts as 'Strange'," she remarked.

Jo's card-house collapsed as a loud *crash* sounded from the hallway. And the card-house wasn't the only thing to fall down – Max lost his grip on the bookcase.

"Whooahh – oooph . . ."

Max struggled out of the comfy chair he'd landed in as Jo, Allie and Timmy all rushed from the study into the hallway. Dylan was sitting at the foot of the stairs, rubbing his head, surrounded by a dozen books. His glasses sat crooked on his nose.

"Ooh," he said groggily.

"Dylan!" Jo said in concern. 'Are you all right?'

"Couldn't see over the pile of books," Dylan mumbled, still rubbing his head. "Now I have a bump."

"Close-up of a bump!" Max exclaimed, struck with inspiration as the others moved to help Dylan up. "It'll look like Mount Everest!" And he snapped off a shot of Dylan's head.

"Ooooh," Dylan moaned, blinking at the ferocity of the flash. "Now I have a bump *and* I'm blind."

"The Case of the Missing Millionaire: an Abelard B. Covington Mystery," Jo read, picking up one of the scattered books and reading the cover.

"He's only seventeen, but he's the world's greatest detective!" Dylan said. His voice oozed with admiration.

"I've heard of him," Max said. "He solves

impossible cases, then he turns them into bestsellers!"

"He's signing his latest bestseller in town tomorrow," Dylan said eagerly. "I bet he's even richer than old man Dunston . . ."

A short distance away, an imposing manor house stood in the evening chill, its gravel drive raked to perfection and a cluster of trees to one side. Standing in the slanting moonlit shadows of the woodland, a dark figure observed the house, whose windows glowed with rich light.

"Dunston Manor," said the figure thoughtfully to himself. "Time to make high-and-mighty Mister Dunston a little less wealthy . . ." And he reached into a kit-bag and produced a crowbar, before padding silently across the wide, soft lawn.

Read the adventures of George and the
original Famous Five in

Five On A Treasure Island
Five Go Adventuring Again
Five Run Away Together
Five Go To Smuggler's Top
Five Go Off In A Caravan
Five On Kirrin Island Again
Five Go Off To Camp
Five Get Into Trouble
Five Fall Into Adventure
Five On A Hike Together
Five Have A Wonderful Time
Five Go Down To The Sea
Five Go To Mystery Moor
Five Have Plenty Of Fun
Five On A Secret Trail
Five Go To Billycock Hill
Five Get Into A Fix
Five On Finniston Farm
Five Go To Demon's Rocks
Five Have A Mystery To Solve
Five Are Together Again

THE
FAMOUS FIVE'S
SURVIVAL GUIDE

includes the NEW Unsolved Mystery

Packed with useful information on surviving outdoors and solving mysteries, here is the one mystery that the Famous Five never managed to solve. See if you can follow the trail to discover the location of the priceless Royal Dragon of Siam.

The perfect book for all fans of mystery, adventure and the Famous Five!

ISBN 9780340970836

LOOK OUT FOR THE WHOLE SERIES!

THE CASE OF THE HOT-AIR
BA-BOOM!

Hodder
Children's
Books

A division of Hachette Children's Books

Special thanks to Lucy Courtenay and Artful Doodlers

Chapter One

A smoky mist was rising off the field in the dim dawn light. Six brightly coloured hot-air balloons stood in a row behind a starting line, waiting for the whistle that would start the Falcongate Three-Day Balloon Race. The only sound was the odd *whoosh* of gas from the balloons' burners, and the surprised moo of cows in the neighbouring meadow.

Four kids and a dog walked among the balloons, ducking beneath tethering ropes and chatting to one another.

"It's too bad we have to go and see my mum get her botany society award today," Jo said, pushing her dark hair off her face. She glanced longingly at

the balloons. "We could've entered this."

"We could've *won*," Jo's cousin Allie said confidently. "Aunt George has a balloon, and Jo knows how to drive it." She fiddled with the long, colourful silk scarf she was wearing so that it flowed more gracefully round her shoulders. "Or float it," she added with a shrug. "Or whatever you do with it."

"I cook with it," Max said cheerfully. He waved a very long toasting fork at the others, on the end of which was a sausage frazzling nicely over a nearby balloon's propane burner.

"If we can't *enter* the race, maybe we could make some money from it," Dylan said thoughtfully. He took off his glasses and started polishing them vigorously – a sign that he was working out the amount of money he might be able to make. "I'll sell the racers snacks," he added, polishing harder. "Everyone loves snacks."

"Wing Commander Bragg certainly does," Max agreed, gesturing towards a large, military-looking balloon in the middle of the field. "He used to be a tough fighter ace, but he does love his food now."

Ramrod-straight retired RAF officer Wing

Commander Bragg was striding round his balloon basket, studying it from various angles along with his short, stout and entirely dependable wife Gertie. Bragg lifted a police whistle to his lips and gave three sharp blasts.

"Roger, dear," his wife Gertie said, snapping out a sharp salute as she responded to the whistle blasts. "Fuel secured. Ballast stowed. And a lovely fried-egg sandwich for you . . ." she added.

As Wing Commander Bragg took his sandwich with evident delight, Max broke off a small piece of

his own freshly cooked sausage and offered it to Timmy. Ignoring the small piece, Timmy jumped up at the rest of the sausage instead, gobbling the entire smoking chunk straight off the fork.

A nervous-looking starter climbed on to a platform in the middle of the field and started studying his clipboard. The atmosphere sharpened at once. It was clear that the race was about to begin.

"Hey, Allie!" drawled a girl's voice from the basket beneath an enormous balloon monogrammed with the letter 'D'. "What's up with the scarf?"

Daine Dunston and her twin brother Blaine were the rich kids of Falcongate, and liked to make sure everyone knew it. The Five tried not to have anything to do with them, but the Dunstons were pretty hard to avoid.

"It was a birthday present," Allie said shortly, twisting her scarf round her shoulders again. "It's Italian."

"Oh," smirked Daine Dunston. "I thought a circus clown had lost his trousers."

"Ha, ha, ha!" Allie said, unamused. "You Dunstons – you're very funny. I hope they land in

an open sewer," she added to Jo as Daine disappeared back into her basket again in a cloud of mocking laughter.

"Hey, Blaine, Daine," Jo shouted up at the monogrammed balloon. "What's the 'D' on your balloon stand for? 'Duh'?"

"Hee, hee – zing!" Allie chuckled, her good humour firmly back in place.

The Starter raised his starting pistol. "Balloonists," he said in rather a weedy voice, "let the Falcongate Three-Day Race begin!" He fiddled with the pistol, wincing and muttering: "Oh, I hate this part . . ." before plugging his ears and firing the pistol into the air.

POP!

One of the balloons exploded into shreds of brightly coloured silk. A second rapidly deflated, lurching wildly through the air with its pilot hanging on to the ropes for dear life. A third balloon snapped all its connecting ropes, leaving a puzzled pilot sitting on the ground in his gondola basket as the balloon part of his equipment sailed into the brightening sky. The Five watched with concern as Wing Commander Bragg's balloon

jerked and began to rise extremely slowly.

"I know, honeypot!" shouted Gertie as Bragg blew his whistle frantically. "The regulator's been sabotaged! We're not getting enough lift."

The Braggs' balloon drifted lazily into the highest branches of a tall tree, its basket snagging on the branches. A string of powerlines hung dangerously close.

"They'll be OK," Jo said, peering anxiously up into the tree. "As long as the wind doesn't push them toward the power lines."

A gust of wind riffled Allie's scarf. The Braggs' gondola basket started to swing towards the power lines.

"Oh, me and my big mouth," Jo muttered, breaking into a sprint with the others close behind.

Chapter Two

The tree where the Braggs were trapped had a wide, rough trunk and several low-hanging branches. The Kirrins quickly started to climb, as Timmy seized the balloon's dangling rope to hold the balloon steady and stop it from swinging anywhere near the power lines.

"Hang on, Mr Bragg – we'll get you loose!" Max called, swiftly climbing the tree after Jo like a blond, good-natured monkey. "I'm good at loosening stuff. My mum always gets me to open jam jars."

As they climbed, one end of Allie's scarf caught on a branch and slipped off her shoulders.

"Shoot . . ." Allie muttered, stopping mid-climb and staring at her scarf with consternation. "Don't rip, don't rip! You're expensive. *Molto* expensive."

She swiped at the dangling end of the scarf with her foot. The scarf wrapped snugly round her ankle. Struggling loose, Allie reached up to free the snagged end, managing to get *that* end wrapped round her wrist.

"I'm turning into a very expensive mummy," Allie wailed as she tried to unwrap her ankle, only tangling the two ends together and wrapping herself up like a brightly coloured parcel halfway up the tree.

Further up the tree, Max, Jo and Dylan arrived level with the Braggs' dangling gondola basket. The power lines sparked menacingly.

"Throw us your anchor rope!" Jo called.

The wing commander tossed a long rope out of the basket. Max wound the rope round a tree limb to increase the leverage, and Jo and Dylan pulled on the rope so that the basket swung over safely into the branches. Straightening her sensible ballooning outfit, Gertie climbed out of the basket, followed by her husband. Leaving the Braggs to

untangle the wreckage of their balloon, Jo, Max and Dylan headed back down to the ground.

On the way down, they passed Allie, who was by now thoroughly trussed up in her scarf and dangling gently from a branch.

"Do you need help, Allie, or are you planning to hatch out as a butterfly?" Dylan asked as they passed.

"Ha, ha," said Allie in an upside-down kind of voice. "Yes, I guess I need help." She wriggled a bit and managed to seize part of the scarf. It instantly unravelled. "Ahhh . . . whoo . . . pa . . ." Allie squealed as she thumped abruptly to the ground. "Oof," she panted, staring at the sky. "No, I guess I don't . . ."

Moments later Max jumped down out of the tree. He found Allie gazing sadly at the tattered remains of her scarf.

"That is why Sir Edmund Hillary didn't wear designer scarves or fancy dresses when he climbed Everest," Max declared, dusting himself down. "Actually," he added with one of his random hand-waves, "I assume he never wore them – but you get my point."

"Allie's a girlie-girl, Max," Dylan explained,

dropping out of the tree with Jo. "Asking her to go outdoors without fashion accessories is like asking a snail not to leave slime."

Appalled, Allie wrinkled her nose. "Ew!" she protested.

Dylan shrugged with an 'I've made my point' gesture.

Allie flared up. "I don't *have* to be so girlie-girl," she snapped.

Her cousins all raised their eyebrows.

"Fine," said Allie defensively. "I'll prove it. I can be tough. I can be as much of a tomboy as Jo."

She seized her scarf and made to tear it in two. She couldn't. Trying harder only got her tangled up all over again.

"Keep trying, Allie," said Jo, amused. "I want to find out what happened to those balloons . . ."

Back on the balloon field a little later, the Kirrins wandered around examining the various bits of balloon wreckage that littered the grass. The balloonists were working hard to repair the damage and get the race started again, but they had a great deal to do.

"The ropes were cut through . . ." Dylan noted of one balloon.

"The propane hose was punctured . . ." Max added, straightening up from examining another.

Allie took up a hose to examine it. She dropped it almost immediately. "Ew, it's got grease all over it!" she wailed, backing away. Then, realising how she would look, she paused and struck a macho pose, trying not to get grease on her outfit. "I mean: hey, it's grease, big whup, huh? Huh? Heh-heh-heh," she stuttered. "Ew," she added in a low voice when she was quite sure the others weren't listening.

"These tapes are all unstitched," said Jo, stepping back from another damaged balloon. "None of this was an accident – these balloons were sabotaged!"

"Who would *do* that?" Max asked in bewilderment. "Who doesn't like *balloons?*"

Jo pointed at the Dunstons' balloon. It was still standing on the start line, looking as pristine as it had before the whole fiasco of the race had begun. "The Dunstons' balloon is fine," she said. "And they always say they'll 'win no matter what'." She

gestured at the wreckage around them. "They could have done this."

"Scarcely matters who did it," said an upright, busybodyish man as he strode past the cousins. "It's dangerous. I didn't sign up to help out with a race to disaster, Mr Starter!"

The busybodyish man marched across to the Starter, who was talking to another bruised-looking balloonist at the side of the field.

The Starter turned round in surprise. "Actually," he stammered, "my name is Tinkerby. Titus Tinkerby."

"That's your misfortune," sniffed the man. "I propose that the race be cancelled. 'Safety first, or fear the worst; safe for one is safe for all'." He paused and straightened his jacket, adding with pride: "From Hugo Leadwell's *Guide to Good Citizenship* – that's *my* book."

There was a fearsome series of hard whistle blasts from Wing Commander Bragg, who was making repairs to his basket nearby.

"I agree with the Wing Commander," said Gertie immediately. "We didn't give up at the Battle of Britain. Why walk away now?"

The Starter scratched his head and looked

12

around at the expectant balloonists. "Hmmm . . ." he said weakly. "Does everyone think they can repair their balloons for a six a.m. start tomorrow?"

"We'll be there!" said Blaine Dunston immediately.

"And so will we!" Jo responded.

The other Kirrins gawped at her.

"We've got my mum's balloon," Jo reminded them. "And there's no botany award tomorrow. Maybe we can find out who's behind this stuff."

"All right!" said Allie in her macho voice. "Let's get 'em! We'll show 'em who's in charge!"

Chapter Three

Back at Jo's house that afternoon, a sturdy-looking gondola basket stood near a colourful, deflated balloon. Jo's dad Ravi was half-in and half-out of the basket as he worked on something inside. As usual, all the kids could see of him was his legs.

"The propane mount is fine," Ravi said in a muffled voice. "I just need a spanner to tighten it."

"Gotcha covered, big guy," Allie declared.

Wearing heavy overalls, Allie cracked her knuckles, flexed her wrist and studied the contents of her toolbelt. There was a pause.

"Is a spanner the twirly thing with teeth," Allie asked in her normal voice, "or the little spinny guy

with two handles and a loop?" She cleared her throat and deepened her voice again as she casually added: "I'll just bring everything . . ."

Leaning down, she grabbed the tool box at her feet. It was so heavy that she moved it approximately half a centimetre before falling over backwards.

"Oooph . . ." Allie mumbled.

As the box was too heavy for her to lift, Allie tried pushing it towards Ravi with her feet. She was almost as unsuccessful with this as she had been with picking it up. Taking pity on her, Timmy trotted over to the box, seized a spanner and took it to Ravi in the gondola basket.

George brought out a bag of sandwiches, which she gave to Max and Jo. Max sniffed the sandwiches approvingly before he stowed them away in the gondola.

"A balloon race," George sighed. "How exciting. When I was a girl, my cousins and I travelled by caravan. It's a fine way to get a good, long look at a horse's rump."

Dylan stepped back from sewing something to the balloon. "Ta-da!" he declared proudly. "An

advert for Constantine's Crazy Golf."

He held up his handiwork. It showed a cartoon of a putter about to strike a golfball.

"Is he paying us for that?" Max asked.

"Course not," Dylan scoffed. "He's paying *me*."

"We're ready to inflate," Ravi called from the gondola basket. "For a change, I won't be the only one full of hot air! I'm making a joke," he added, just in case.

And with a whoosh of propane, the balloon began to fill.

Early the next morning, the cousins were floating in George's balloon high up in the sky over Falcongate. Six other balloons hovered nearby, all following the course of a river down below. In one corner of the basket, Jo plotted a course on a map as the balloon coasted gently on the air currents. In another, Allie struggled to do exercises with a barbell.

"Ungh . . . ungh . . . phew!" Allie groaned. "How do people do this?"

She unscrewed the collar at one end of the barbell, unaware that the collar at the other end was

sliding off. As it fell over the side of the basket, the
rest of the weights followed, plummeting to the
ground. Max leaned out and watched the weights
fall in front of the Falcongate post office.

"Well," he said after a minute. "Now we know a
postbox can't stand up to a five-kilo weight."

"Take a look at the Braggs . . ." called Dylan from
behind his video camera.

Through his zoom lens, Dylan could see the
Braggs in their balloon. They appeared to be doing
some kind of balloon drill. Bragg blew his whistle;

17

Gertie saluted and marched to the right two steps to tie a knot. Bragg blew his whistle again; Gertie saluted, marched left one step, moved a crate a half-metre along the bottom of the basket and saluted again.

Getting bored, Dylan panned across the sky to another balloon. He stopped and stared intently. "There's something interesting in the Dunstons' balloon . . ." he said.

Jo sat up, alert. "What? What?"

Dylan adjusted the focus on his camera. "They've got a mini-fridge, and a massage chair, a TV and – wow – a satellite dish!"

"Really?" said Max, perking up. "What are they watching? Something with aliens?"

"Figure skating," said Dylan after a pause.

Allie gasped with excitement. "Is it pairs?"

The others looked at her.

"I mean, yuk," Allie said quickly. "Chick stuff."

"Hey, Kirrins!" Blaine Dunston yelled across, putting his head out of his gondola basket. "Are you still limping along in that vintage gasbag? Show them how the Dunstons do it, Daine."

Daine leaned over the back of the basket and

switched on a high-powered fan. The Dunstons' balloon leaped forward like a startled beachball and whizzed on ahead.

"See you at the finish line!" Daine yelled over the back of the basket.

"Oh, no you don't . . ." Jo snarled.

She reached up to turn down the propane flow to the burner. George's balloon began to sink.

"Jo, this isn't faster," Allie said kindly, "this is lower. We want faster. Faster, faster!"

Jo made some minute adjustments. "Wait till we get into that gorge . . ." she said.

The balloon descended into a rocky gorge with a river running through it like a silver thread. Instantly, it was rocketed forward by the gusty winds that were tearing along the gorge.

"Whoa . . ." Allie squealed, hanging on for safety, "this *is* faster!"

"Much faster," Dylan panted. "And, if I might add – *yikes!*"

He pointed at a huge tree growing out of the side of the gorge. The balloon was racing straight towards it!

"Shovel," Jo said calmly, holding out her hand.

Allie handed Jo the small shovel. Jo thrust the handle through a metal loop on the rim of the basket and used the shovel as a rudder, steering the balloon round the tree and then dodging rocky outcrops on each side of the gorge.

"I'm thirsty," Max announced. He pointed at an approaching waterfall. "Could you steer that way please?"

Jo obligingly headed close to the waterfall, allowing Max to hold out a glass and fill it up with splashing, sparkling water. Timmy hung out of the basket and lapped at the waterfall as they zipped past.

"I don't mean to be Mr Yikes here," Dylan croaked, "but – *yikes!*"

Now the balloon was heading towards the end of the gorge, where the gorge walls narrowed to a bottle neck. There was no way the balloon was going to fit through the rocks.

"*Now* we want higher. Faster no good. Higher better." Allie squeaked.

Jo turned the propane back up with a flick of her wrist. But just as the balloon started to ascend, it bumped into something above it. The Dunstons

had positioned their gondola basket right above the Five's balloon, keeping it from rising out of the gorge.

"Looks like you're trapped down there," Daine called down merrily. "Hope you have a 'smashing' time!"

Daine and Blaine laughed and high-fived each other, not noticing that they had headed right into a patch of vines growing on the top of the gorge. The vines were sucked into the Dunstons' fan blades in an instant, wrapping round the machinery and burning out the motor with a fizz and lots of extremely smelly smoke.

As the Dunstons rushed to disentangle themselves, the Five's balloon drifted clear of the Dunstons'. Jo cranked up the propane, and the balloon soared up out of the gorge not a minute too soon.

"See ya at the finish line!" Allie yelled at the Dunstons. She looked pleased, adding: "It's kind of fun being a macho jerk, sometimes."

Jo shut down the burner as the balloon drifted on through the clear sky. "Max," she said, "could you climb up inside the envelope and make sure the

21

parachute valve is completely shut?"

Max shrugged, not moving. "Of course I could!" he said agreeably, getting more comfortable in the basket. "Easy!"

"Could you do it now?" Jo added, raising her eyebrows.

Max scrambled to his feet. "Oh! Aye-aye, Jo . . ."

He clambered up so he could see up into the balloon. Fastened high inside was a nest of straw, which contained a small vial of clear liquid. Attached by wires to the bottom of the nest was a magnifying lens, angled to direct heat from the burners to the straw. The straw was starting to smoulder.

"Jo," Max called over his shoulder. "Is there supposed to be a magnifying glass setting fire to a pile of straw in here?"

"No," Jo said slowly.

"Then we've been booby-trapped," Max said, scrambling backwards very fast. "If we don't do something quickly, we're going to crash!"

Chapter Four

Max did his best to describe the device without panicking out loud.

"It's almost like a bird's nest with some sort of liquid inside," he gabbled.

"It's probably flammable," Jo said. "If it catches fire, the whole balloon will go up like a torch."

Dylan swallowed. "And I'm not wearing any sunscreen," he said unhappily.

The straw flickered. A tiny flame could now be seen. Max stretched out his arm, but the device was just beyond his fingertips.

"I can't put out the fire; I can't reach it!" he shouted.

Allie rummaged through her rucksack and produced a spray bottle. "Here," she said, tossing the bottle to Max. "It's floral water."

Max seized the bottle and pressed the nozzle. It sent a steady stream of water up at the smouldering straw, extinguishing it.

"And once again, beauty products save the day," Allie declared happily.

The others rolled their eyes.

"Hey," Allie protested, "I am *going* tomboy, but . . . one step at a time."

Jo fiddled with the propane burner. "We have to shut down the burner or that thing could catch fire again," she explained, as the propane hissed and fell silent.

"But we'll fall behind," Dylan objected.

"It's only the first leg of the race," Jo reminded him. "We're near the finishing point anyway. But hang on tight – the landing might be a little bumpy . . ."

Down in a wooded field, Hugo Leadwell, author of Hugo Leadwell's *Guide to Good Citizenship* and an assortment of other small publications, studied the sky with his binoculars.

WALLOP!

Leadwell stumbled backwards into a bramble bush as the Five's balloon dropped out of the sky and hit him.

"Owww!" he howled.

"Told you," Jo said to her cousins with a shrug.

Later that afternoon, Hugo Leadwell's truck pulled into the race encampment, which consisted of a few tents and a larger Race Officials' marquee. In the back of the truck was an assortment of camping equipment, a gondola basket, George's folded balloon and the Five themselves.

"Sorry again that we bonked you with our basket, Mr Leadwell," said Max as he and the others unloaded the camping supplies and equipment.

Leadwell fingered a small bandage on his forehead. "Gave me a chance to use my first aid kit," he said in a fatherly voice. "'A proper citizen is always prepared, so a bonk on the bonce won't make him scared.' Hugo Leadwell, *Poems for Good Citizens*."

Dylan glanced around the encampment. "I think we should get our tent set up."

As they dragged their gear towards the other tents, Leadwell called out: "Whether dining on parsnip or dining on bean, a proper citizen leaves his camp clean." Then he gave them a little salute and headed off.

"Please," said Dylan, "nobody get me his little rhyming book for Christmas."

Allie cracked her knuckles. She was getting better at it. "I'll set up camp," she announced. She pointed at a bundle. "What's that?"

"That's a wondrous device called a 'tent'," Jo explained.

Allie nodded seriously. "'Tent'. Check. I'm all over this." She loaded herself up with the gear and struggled towards a clearing.

Jo produced the booby-trap from the balloon and showed it to the others. "So what do we make of this?" she asked.

Max took the small vial of liquid from Jo and sniffed it. "Doesn't smell like gas or paraffin," he said. "Doesn't smell like chocolate. Doesn't smell like a lot of things."

"My science teacher made ethanol last term," said Dylan, studying the bottle. "It was clear like that."

"Well, that would burn up my mum's balloon pretty well," Jo said. "And paying for it would've come out of *my* pocket money."

"And we would've fallen a thousand metres out of the sky," Dylan pointed out, looking a little green. "I put it to you that *that* would sting."

In the background, Allie struggled to unroll an air mattress. She produced a small, battery-operated pump and attached the airhose to the mattress, looking pleased with herself. Then she switched on the pump. It quickly inflated the mattress to the point where the mattress flew off the end of the hose and careered around in the air, deflating loudly as it went. Allie dived out of the way as the mattress sailed overhead and got lodged in some tree branches.

"I bet the Dunstons are behind this," Jo continued, still studying the vial of ethanol.

"Let's check their tent," Max suggested. "Dylan – you and Timmy distract them."

Allie had now managed to unroll their dome tent. She quickly ran the flexible pole through the outside roof loops and bent the pole to stand the tent up. Struggling to bend it double, she lost her

grip and ended up catapulting the tent into the same tree that the air mattress had landed in.

"Executive decision," Allie panted, mopping her forehead. "We're camping in that tree tonight."

Dylan strolled casually through the camp with Timmy, trying to find the Dunstons and prevent them from returning to their tent before Max and Jo had finished searching it for evidence. At last he spotted them walking along.

"Blaine!" he shouted, following them. "Daine!"

The twins glanced round.

"Can you help?" Dylan improvised. "We sat in nettles!"

He scratched himself, twisting and contorting to reach various remote spots on his body. Timmy scratched obligingly beside him, scooting along the ground with the effort.

The Dunstons pointed and laughed. Dylan flung himself around a little more wildly, and they laughed some more.

"Well," said Blaine, grinning, "as entertaining as that is, I guess we'll go to our tent."

"Ow!" Dylan said, thinking fast. "Now I've

stubbed my toe! Ow-ow-ow-ow . . ."

He hopped around in feigned pain and bumped into the Dunstons' tent. Distracted, the Dunstons roared with laughter again.

Jo and Max peered round the edge of the Dunstons' tent. When they were sure that the Dunstons weren't looking their way, they ducked inside.

The Dunstons' tent was the last word in luxury. It had photos of the Dunston family everywhere, a drinks machine and a large-screen TV in one corner. Jo looked inside a rucksack.

"Ah-ha!" she said triumphantly. "Matches, barbecue lighter fluid, a magnifying glass. Pretty suspicious, huh?"

Max scratched his head. "Um," he said, "it's kind of standard camping stuff. I mean, we have all that."

Jo put her hands on her hips. "Max," she said in annoyance, "whose side are you on?"

Outside the tent, Dylan had now managed to get himself covered in ashes, and was coughing and sneezing for the Dunstons' benefit.

"I can't believe I fell in the ashes of that old

29

campfire," Dylan panted. "Yuk!"

Daine shrugged, and glanced at her brother. "I think the entertainment value's wearing off," she said in a bored voice. "Let's go."

They started towards the door of their tent.

"Um . . ." Dylan said desperately. "Timmy?"

Timmy leaped on to Blaine and Daine, knocking them to the ground and licking their faces enthusiastically.

"Look at that," Dylan said. "He likes you. He can keep that up for hours," he added cheerfully.

"Maybe even all night. Well, see you."

"Yuk!" Daine wailed.

"Get off me!" howled Blaine.

But Timmy took no notice.

Chapter Five

Up in the sky the next day, the balloons were once again aloft in the Falcongate Three-Day Race. Allie, in her most tomboyish outfit, gnawed bravely on something tough and leathery as Jo tinkered with the balloon's propane burner.

"Rrggh," Allie mumbled. "Mmmmmph!" Giving up, she lowered the thing she was trying to chew. "Sheesh, Jo, how can you eat pork scratchings?" she complained, looking at the object in her hand with disgust. "They're like shoe leather."

"That *is* shoe leather," Jo said kindly. "I always bring extra insoles for my hiking boots. The pork scratchings are in that rucksack."

Allie gazed at her snack in dismay. Then, determined to be tough, she continued chewing anyway, making fierce "Ung, yum, yum-yum" noises.

The Braggs' military-style balloon drifted past.

"Morning, Commander!" Max shouted cheerfully, snapping out a salute. "How are you and Mrs Bragg today?"

Bragg responded with a series of whistle blasts.

"We're fine!" Gertie shouted back. "But some scoundrel cut through the bottom of our basket, and we're about to plummet to our doom. Tally-ho."

RRRIPPP!

The floor of the Braggs' gondola basket gave way, sending the Braggs plummeting downwards. As they fell, parachutes billowed open from their backpacks. The sound of Wing Commander Bragg's whistle floated thinly on the air, followed by Gertie shouting: "Yes, dear, you have told me about the time you parachuted behind enemy lines. Many times."

The Braggs' empty balloon drifted onwards as the Five looked at each other.

"They might be better off than us," Jo remarked. "Look what's heading our way . . ."

She pointed ahead to a dark storm cloud. It began to rain hard, with high winds screaming around the balloon and lightning that stabbed through the air.

"We've got to land!" Jo shouted over the wind. *"Now!"*

As Max pulled the parachute valve cord to let air out and Jo turned down the burner, Dylan shouted over to the Dunstons in their balloon:

"Get out of the sky! It's too dangerous!"

"You get out of the sky, Nettle Boy!" Blaine sneered. "See you at the finish line!"

There was a blinding flash of lightning. The Dunstons' balloon shivered and began to descend rapidly.

"We're going down!" Daine wailed. "I'm going to have Daddy sue the weatherman!"

The Dunstons' balloon sank like a stone, heading straight for a farm down below. With a squelch, they landed hard in a pig sty, sinking deep into the mud.

The Five's balloon landed safely nearby. The cousins hopped out of their basket and raced over to the sty, where the Dunstons were furiously

wiping mud off themselves.

"Well, well, well," Max grinned, helping to drag the Dunstons' basket out of the muck. "Looks like Karma has paid a little visit. You guys sabotaged people and it came back to bite you. Cosmic justice."

Jo examined the inside of the Dunstons' basket. "No," she said after a minute, "they didn't sabotage people."

"Jo, whose side are you on?" Max complained.

"Not theirs," said Jo. "But their propane hose has been cut through. They were sabotaged, too."

Still waist-deep in pig muck, the Dunstons struggled to get out of the sty.

"Give me a leg up," Blaine ordered Daine.

"*You* give *me* a leg up . . ." Daine screamed straight back.

As they scuffled with each other, they slipped and fell back into the mud, grunting as they went under the brown ooze.

"Not that they don't deserve it . . ." Jo added.

Chapter Six

Once again, Hugo Leadwell and his truck came to the rescue. Both balloon rigs were loaded into the back, with the help of the Five. Needless to say, the Dunstons just stood back and glared.

Once the rigs were stashed in the back, Hugo Leadwell pulled an unusual-looking knife from his pocket and cut a length of rope. Setting the knife down, he then used the rope to tie down the rigs to stop them falling out of the truck on the way back to the camp.

"Thanks for giving us a lift, buddy," Allie said, making an attempt at a jaunty tomboy laugh and slapping Leadwell on the back.

Max picked up Hugo Leadwell's knife. It was deadly sharp, and its handle was made of yellowed horn with odd grooves and ridges on it. "Don't forget your pocketknife, Mr Leadwell!" he called. "'Leadwell Farms . . . Symond Valley'," he read on the knife handle as he handed it over. "Cool logo, my safety-minded friend."

"I'm very proud of my farm," said Hugo Leadwell, pocketing the knife. "A thousand acres of maize, pretty as a beauty queen." He cleared his throat, which was always a sign that he was about to quote from one of his many community-minded publications. " 'A citizen's land should be tidy and trim – he protects it, and the law protects him.' "

"For someone who's such a 'law-abiding citizen', he has a very illegal knife," Max whispered to the others as Hugo Leadwell went back to fastening the balloons in place. "The handle is rhinoceros horn – it's totally banned."

"How do you know it's rhinoceros?" Dylan whispered back.

Max shrugged. "I did a school project on endangered species. Rhino horn has these squiggly things on it." He made squiggly motions with his

fingers to indicate the unusual patterns on the knife handle.

"So it's no ordinary scout knife," Jo said thoughtfully. "Maybe Mr Leadwell isn't what he seems either . . ."

Back in the balloon camp that evening, Hugo Leadwell strode among the tents, nodding to the balloonists that were camped out on all sides. As he passed a clump of bushes, the heads of the Five popped out and watched his progress. Stealthily, Jo, Max, Dylan, Allie – squeezing hard on a pair of grip-strengtheners – and Timmy set off on his tail.

They followed Leadwell to the Officials' Tent. Waiting until Leadwell had disappeared through the tent flaps, they gathered on the outside of the canvas to eavesdrop on the conversation.

"Cancel the race?" came the Starter's voice. He didn't sound happy. "Dear me . . ."

"Look," said Leadwell urgently, "I'm just a simple farmer, but all these accidents just don't smell right."

"You know," Dylan whispered to the others outside the tent, "ethanol can be made from maize." He looked pleased. "My science teacher will be

very happy her experiment had practical value. I'll have to send her a postcard."

"Letting these balloons back up would be lunacy," Leadwell continued. "I insist you mustn't send them over Symond Valley when someone is trying to sabotage them."

"Symond Valley," Max said, dropping all thoughts of amusing cows. "That's where his farm is. Unless his knife was lying."

"Maize makes ethanol," Jo deduced. "We were nearly sabotaged by ethanol. And he doesn't want anyone flying over his farm."

"I think we should see what he's trying to hide," Allie said, still working hard on her grip-strengtheners.

Jo nodded, adding: "And I don't think we should wait for anyone's permission . . ."

There was a pinging sound. Allie's grip-strengtheners flew from her grasp and disappeared over the Starter's tent.

"Oooh . . ." said Allie helplessly.

"Owwww!"

Blaine and Daine Dunston, on their way back to their luxurious tent, both rubbed their heads and

stared in confusion at the grip-strengtheners lying on the grass at their feet.

"Nice shot, Allie," said Dylan in approval.

Chapter Seven

Half an hour later, the light had faded from the sky. The encampment was lit by the flickering glow of campfires and torches. And back in the Starter's tent, Hugo Leadwell and the Starter were still deep in conversation.

"The race is scheduled to resume at sunrise," said the Starter. "I have till then to decide whether to cancel it."

"I hope you make the right decision," Leadwell said gravely. He cleared his throat in that now-familiar manner. "If you leap before you look, it may your own goose you cook." Cocking his head, he considered something for a moment before

admitting: "That one needs a little work."

Saluting the Starter meaningfully, Leadwell ducked out of the tent and headed back across the camp. Passing the Five's tent, he glanced at the shadows that the cousins were casting against the canvas from the inside. A rousing chorus of *Mairi's Wedding* filtered through the tent flaps and into the evening air.

"Step we gaily, on we go," boomed the voices. *"Heel for heel and toe for toe, Arm in arm and row on row, all for Mairi's wedding . . ."*

Leadwell grunted, then continued on his way. Behind him, the torchlight flickered against the five cardboard cut-outs in the Five's tent and Dylan's MP3 player continued cheerfully blasting the song through his laptop speakers. And over Leadwell's head, the Kirrins' balloon rose silently above the treetops and climbed away into the night.

A full moon illuminated the Five in their balloon as they glided along.

"So," Jo said, peering over the edge of the gondola basket, "the sabotage wasn't to help

someone win – it was to make sure nobody got this far . . ."

"And people might call me overly suspicious," Max said, pointing down, "but I'm guessing that's the reason why."

Far below the balloon lay an immense tract of land. Its perimeter was neatly lined with stalks of maize, and to the average passer-by on the small country roads that wound around the property, all was as it should be. But from their vantage point in the sky, the Five had a very different picture of Symond Valley. Within the perimeter of maize, the entire property was a jungle-like expanse of lakes, streams and trees, all ringed with double barbed-wire fences.

"In America," Allie remarked, "maize farms just grow maize."

"Most of them here do too," Jo said. She made some adjustments to the propane burner. "Next stop – jungle."

Jo pulled the parachute cord, and the balloon began to descend.

The lakes glimmered in the moonlight. The trees, which had looked dark and forbidding from

high up in the sky, looked increasingly jungle-like as the balloon drifted towards them. As Jo set the balloon down on the ground, the moonlight disappeared abruptly, cut off by the high treetops.

"I hope the batteries in my torch are working," Max muttered. "I hope I have batteries in my torch. I hope I even have my torch."

"I think that flaming arrow will provide plenty of light . . ." Dylan squeaked.

Sure enough, a blazing arrow was speeding towards the balloon out of the gloom. Instinctively, the kids ducked. The arrow ripped its way through the balloon, setting it ablaze.

"Ginger beer," Max shouted, tossing cans of fizzy drinks to the others from the supplies in the smoking gondola basket. "Quick!"

"I'm not really thirsty . . ." Allie began, catching her ginger beer in some confusion.

Ignoring his cousin, Max shook his can vigorously, opened it and sprayed ginger beer over the flames. The others did the same. Within moments, the fire was doused. The balloon, which now had a gaping charred hole in its side, collapsed in a deflated heap.

"Well," Jo said glumly, staring at the wreckage, "there goes a year's worth of pocket money . . ."

"Now we're stuck," Max said. He scratched his head as he stared at the charred remains of the balloon. "And someone doesn't seem very happy we're here."

The roar of an angry lion filled the air. The Five whirled round. Now there was the distinctive trumpeting of an irritated elephant, followed by the howl of a hungry hyena.

Dylan jumped as a giant anaconda slithered past them on a long tree branch. "I can't say I'm that tickled about it myself," he gulped.

Chapter Eight

The Five stood tensely in the darkness, listening to the weird and frightening night sounds of jungle animals on the prowl around them. Timmy barked, only to be answered by a deep-throated growl.

"That was definitely a tiger," Dylan said.

The growling quietened. In its place, something laughed wildly.

"And *that's* a hyena," Dylan added.

"I hope they eat you," came a petulant voice from the Five's gondola basket.

"I hope they eat *you*," came a second voice from inside the basket as well.

"And *that*," said Jo, whirling round, "was a couple of rats . . ."

She looked into the balloon basket and whisked away a blanket. Crouched underneath, looking scared and angry, were the Dunstons.

"We couldn't let you get to the finish line before us," Daine said sulkily, brushing imaginary blanket fluff off her cashmere jumper. "We have to be first at everything."

RAAARRGH!

47

Another roar penetrated the gloom of the trees. Everyone jumped.

"Great," Jo said. "You can be the first to get eaten."

The burly gamekeeper paced up and down outside Hugo Leadwell's house, his hunting bow hanging loose in one hand and his mobile phone in the other. A quiver of arrows rested on his back.

"Yeah, Mr Leadwell," he said in a strong Australian accent. "I brought down the balloon with a 'hot' arrow. But the kids are still loose on the property."

On the other end of the phone, Leadwell sounded furious. "We've got four big game hunters arriving tomorrow to go after rhino. You'd better have those kids accounted for by then."

"Shall I just open up the cages?" suggested the gamekeeper.

"Good idea," Leadwell growled. "The carnivores will solve our problem for us."

Sniggering nastily, Leadwell snapped his phone shut. Throwing one last angry glance at the five

cardboard cut-outs he had found, he pushed his way out of the Five's tent and headed for his truck.

Back in the jungle clearing, the Dunstons looked about with distaste. Blaine stared at the muddy ground and curled his lip, while Daine fussed about with her hair.

"Why did you bring us here?" Daine pouted at Jo. "There's no restaurant, there's no spa, there's no shopping."

"No," Dylan admitted. "But there *is* a tiger . . ."

He pointed. A tiger leaped from a bush in a blur of brown and orange, heading straight towards them. Timmy barked furiously, and the tiger paused just long enough for Allie to give the Dunstons a quick shove up a nearby tree. Max grabbed Dylan and dragged him into the undergrowth, where they both broke into a run. As the tiger whirled around, trying to decide what to chase first, Jo plunged into the jungle with Timmy hot on her heels.

"Get *up* there," Allie panted, pushing hard at the Dunstons.

"I'll ruin my nails . . ." Daine wailed.

The tiger made a decision. It headed towards Allie, who felt its hot and smelly breath on her back.

"GET UP THAT TREE!" Allie screamed. "HUP! HUP!"

Shoving hard, she forced Blaine and Daine up the tree ahead of her and leaped up behind them just as the tiger jumped – and missed.

"This macho stuff can be fun . . ." Allie panted, pleased with herself as the tiger shook its orange head in disappointment.

Max and Dylan were still running. They were heading for a river.

"Crocodiles ahead!" Max shouted. "Big teeth!"

Indeed, three crocodiles were floating like logs in the river.

The boys' momentum carried them pell-mell down the slope towards the water. "Woaaahhhh . . ." they shouted.

"Too steep!" Dylan yelled, his feet moving in a blur. "Can't stop! Watch step!"

Still running, Max and Dylan leaped off the river bank and landed squarely on the crocodiles' backs.

There was no choice but to use the crocs as stepping stones and hope. They pelted on across the river, arriving on the far bank at a cluster of boulders. Scrambling over the boulders, they took a couple of flying leaps – and found themselves on the back of a very surprised rhinoceros. The rhino promptly broke into a run, with the boys clinging helplessly to its back.

"This isn't an improvement . . ." Max panted.

Jo and Timmy ran on through the jungle, and reached a crevasse blocking their escape. Jo sat down against a tree near the edge of the crevasse with Timmy beside her, scanning the surrounding area. She produced a compass and studied it, angling it so that Timmy could see.

"That's north," Jo said, glancing off to the horizon. "So we came from the east . . ."

A huge snake glided slowly towards Timmy from behind. It silently slid under Timmy's midsection and wrapped itself about him like a thick, leathery rope. Before Timmy could react with a bark, the snake had wound itself round his muzzle and silenced him.

"Mff," Timmy barked in an urgent, muffled voice.
"Mff, mff!"

Chapter Nine

Still perched high in the tree, Allie produced a set of binoculars from her rucksack and peered off into the distance.

"My jeans are ruined," Blaine whined from his position higher up the tree branch. "I'll send you the bill."

"And I'll tear it up," Allie replied. She adjusted the focus on her binoculars. A rustic building on a distant hill came into view. "Hey, what's that?" she said. She made a couple more adjustments to the focus. "There's a hunting lodge," she declared. "We'd all be safe there."

Producing a whistle from her rucksack, Allie

began blowing short and long blasts on it.

"If you're trying to hail a taxi, it's not going to work," Blaine said sulkily.

"It's Morse code," said Allie between blasts. "I'm telling my cousins to head to the northeast corner of this crazy place."

"Tell them to bring some bug spray," Daine begged, slapping wildly at her face. "I'm getting eaten by mosquitoes."

Blaine smirked at his sister's discomfort. "Ha ha!" he taunted.

Daine turned and slapped her brother hard on the forehead.

"Oww!" Blaine howled.

"Oh," said Daine sweetly, "there was one on you . . ."

The rhino was still charging. Max and Dylan were still holding on by their fingertips.

"Pond coming up," Max panted, peering over the rhino's horny grey shoulder. "I don't see any crocodiles."

"Meets *my* standards for a good pond . . ." Dylan puffed.

As the rhino thundered past the water, the boys leaped off and landed with a splash in the pond. They surfaced, spluttering, to the sound of Allie's whistle drifting towards them.

Elsewhere in the jungle, Jo was struggling to pry the snake's long brown coils off Timmy. It was no easy task. No sooner had she removed one coil than the snake had flung out another.

"Hang on, Timmy," Jo said, as Timmy whined unhappily. "I've got some shampoo in my rucksack . . ."

Rummaging through her bag, she produced a bottle of shampoo and squirted it on Timmy's coat near the snake's tightest coils.

"This ought to slick you up," Jo promised.

She grabbed hold of Timmy's collar and pulled, just as the snake put on an extra squeeze. With a woof of surprise, Timmy shot out of the reptile's coils like a wet bar of soap.

"There," Jo said as Timmy landed safely in a bush. The snake slithered off, looking disgruntled. "Don't complain so much next time I give you a bath."

Timmy leaped on to Jo and licked her face gratefully as Allie's whistle floated through the air towards them.

Back in the tree, Allie put her whistle back in the rucksack. "Time for us to get going," she announced.

Daine's eyes nearly popped out of her head. "*Excuse* me?" she said. "There's still a tiger down there!"

Allie pulled her long, brightly coloured scarf from her pocket and wound it round a branch. After testing it for strength, she seized the free end and swung across to another tree. She let go of the scarf, and it swung back to the Dunstons. Down below, the tiger prowled and stared hungrily upwards.

"That's the way it works," Allie called. "You can follow me or stay there."

Blaine swallowed and took the end of the scarf. Daine grabbed her brother round the waist and hung on when Blaine leaped clumsily off the branch.

As they swung, Blaine's waistband gave way. His trousers slithered down to his ankles, taking Daine

with them and revealing an embarrassing pair of boxer shorts. Daine meanwhile smacked straight into the oncoming tree trunk.

"Owww," Daine wailed.

Observing, Allie shook her head. "You guys are going to *have* to get better at this," she tutted.

The sun was peeping over the horizon as the exhausted kids clambered up to the front of the hunting lodge from all different directions.

"Are we all here?" Jo asked, standing with the others on the hunting lodge's porch. She smiled as Allie appeared with the Dunstons trailing behind her. "Brilliant job getting us to safety, Allie."

Allie looked proud.

They pushed open the door of the hunting lodge and stepped inside. Leadwell and his gamekeeper looked up from the zebra-skin rug in front of the fire, their hunting bows slung over their shoulders.

"No offence, Allie," Jo said, freezing to the spot, "but I'm retracting my previous compliment."

Chapter Ten

Leadwell's face split into an ugly grin as he stared at the six dishevelled kids and the dog in his doorway.

"You had to come snooping around," he growled, taking a step towards them. "You had to find out that I charge big game hunters to stalk endangered species."

"Actually, we didn't know that last bit," Dylan protested. He paused. "*That* would be the illegal bit," he said after a moment. Backing towards the door, he added as breezily as he could manage: "Well, got to go . . ."

"You're not going anywhere," Leadwell snapped.

"*You* are," Jo said boldly. She glanced down at her dog. "Timmy?"

Timmy grabbed the zebra rug in his mouth and pulled it out from under Leadwell and his gamekeeper.

"Ooopphh," grunted the villains, crashing hard to the ground as the kids fled from the lodge and plunged back into the jungle.

Allie led the way. They sprinted along a jungle path, where Allie paused to drop her silk scarf. At a fork in the trail a little further along, she produced a lip gloss from her rucksack and dropped that as well.

"They'll find us," Dylan complained, glancing over his shoulder as they ran on.

"That's the idea . . ." said Allie mysteriously, setting down her open compact so that the mirror glinted in the sunshine.

Leadwell and the gamekeeper struggled to their feet and raced after the kids. They spotted the scarf almost immediately. Then the lip gloss. As they saw the shining mirror and hurried towards it, they stepped neatly in a pair of vine nooses laid on the

ground. The nooses instantly pulled taut and rocketed upwards, leaving Leadwell and his accomplice dangling upside down.

"Aiiiieeee!" they yelled.

"I made some traps in case the tiger followed us," Allie explained.

"We're going to call the police," Dylan informed Leadwell. "Hang around."

"See if you can come up with a rhyme for 'going to jail'," Max added cheerfully.

"Allie, I'm retracting my retraction," Jo said. "Good job."

She slapped Allie heartily on the back.

"Ow!" Allie wailed. "Every bit of me hurts. Every bit of me smells bad . . ." She stepped backwards into another tiger noose. "Whoa!" Now hanging upside down, Allie continued without drawing breath: "Every bit of me is turned upside down . . . Jo, I'm leaving the tomboy stuff to you. I'm going back to being a girlie-girl."

She reached down to the ground and picked up her lip gloss. Lovingly, she kissed it and applied it with a gusty sigh of relief.

* * *

Back in the jungle clearing a little while later, Allie adjusted her neatly pressed blouse and skirt, checking her make-up carefully in her mirror. Constable Stubblefield was leading away the handcuffed Leadwell and his gamekeeper, who were both still looking a little woozy from their stint upside down.

"We're taking this lot out by helicopter," Constable Stubblefield called over her shoulder to the kids. "Would you five care for a lift?"

"Actually, there's seven," Jo began, looking about

61

before she realised that Blaine and Daine Dunston were nowhere to be seen. "Hey," she said in surprise, "when did the Gruesome Twosome sneak off? And where to?"

In a field some distance away, a checkered banner marked the end of the Falcongate Three-Day Balloon Race. The Dunstons, looking much the worse for wear, staggered up to the banner on their hands and knees, feebly clutching a birthday balloon, before collapsing at the surprised Starter's feet.

"We're here," Blaine mumbled, lifting his face from the dirt. "We win."

"We have a balloon, so technically we're balloonists," Daine panted, pushing her sweaty hair out of her eyes.

The Starter shook his head. He started folding up the chair and card table he had been using. "No winners," he said. "The race was cancelled this morning."

The *chock-chock-chock* of helicopter blades overhead made the Dunston twins look up. The Five leaned out of the chopper and waved.

"You guys were right," Max shouted, "you *did* beat us to the finish line!"

"Have a nice walk home!" Dylan laughed.

And Blaine and Daine watched helplessly as the helicopter angled away into the sky and was gone.

Epilogue

The following day, Dylan, Max, Allie and Timmy gathered in George's greenhouse. It was Allie's turn to operate Dylan's video camera and capture more top tips for Dylan's video collection. The greenhouse had been deemed the best place to film for its steamy jungle atmosphere.

"Sticky Situation Number Eight," Allie announced, staggering a little under the weight of the camera. "You Happen Upon A Tiger."

On cue, Dylan and Max emerged from some potted palms wearing pith helmets. Timmy, a tiger skin draped over him, emerged from behind some other potted plants and growled convincingly.

Dylan tipped back his pith helmet and turned to the camera. "If you encounter a tiger," he said, "don't approach it, but don't run away either. That will make you look like prey."

"Instead," Max added, "try to show the animal you're bigger than it is."

He held his jacket up over his head, making himself appear much taller. Dylan meanwhile waved a stick for a similar effect. Timmy growled uncertainly.

"Timmy," Jo called, appearing at the greenhouse door. "Your dinner's ready!"

Abandoning all pretence at being a tiger, Timmy happily bounded away.

"It also helps if the tiger is really just a hungry dog," Max said to the camera after a pause. "Then you're sitting pretty." He sat down, instantly leaping up again. "But I just sat on a cactus," he added, his eyes watering with pain as he hopped around the greenhouse pulling thorns out of his backside. *"Don't* do that. Ow! Ow! *Ow!"*